If you met Jeff and Jenny while they were staying on their grandfather's chinchilla ranch in Colorado, you probably feel they are your good friends. Now, go with them to Alaska for more exciting adventures!

───────────────●───────────────

Jeff was startled when the airline stewardess called him by name and seemed to know they were the twin children of Astronaut Rollins. To his own surprise, he ended up giving her something he treasured, and later he was very glad he did.

───────────────●───────────────

Then Rickey Welch bounded into their lives—all the way from his home in Chile. And life became more lively in the Rollins household.

───────────────●───────────────

There was that accident on the ski slope and Jenny's own problem on the toboggan. But when their precious birthday present from Colorado went astray, the Rollins twins had their Christian values stretched to their limit.

───────────────●───────────────

Jeff & Jenny
Winter in Alaska

Nellie Frisinger

ACCENT BOOKS
Denver, Colorado

Second Printing, 1978

Third Printing, 1984

ACCENT BOOKS,
A division of Accent Publications, Inc.
12100 W. Sixth Avenue
P.O. Box 15337
Denver, Colorado 80215

Library of Congress Catalog Card Number: 77-81775

ISBN 0-916406-82-2

The Jeff & Jenny
ADVENTURE SERIES

Contents

Jeff ...

How do we feel when a friend disappoints us? Jeff felt this way about an older boy very important to him.

But later he learned that God could work a miracle and God let Jeff have a part in it.

Jenny...

Someone was very mean to Jenny—very mean. But Jenny paid her back by helping her when she needed it.

Then God used Jenny's kindness to make something wonderful happen.

FIRE!

JEFF ROLLINS sat tensely on the edge of the car seat.

"Grandpa!" His voice was strained and his throat felt tight. "Grandpa, something is wrong at the ranch!" Jeff tried to peer through the darkness as the Rollins' car hurried along the highway. "Grandpa!" Jeff screamed. "The chinchilla unit is on *fire!* My chinchillas, Sparky and Matilda! They are going to burn up!"

Grandpa's face looked white, his lips were pulled across his teeth. "I see, son, I see," he said softly.

The car was going faster. As they turned into their driveway Jeff heard the wail of a siren and saw flashing red lights behind them. The car stopped suddenly. He held his breath as a huge fire engine shot past. He looked up and saw ominous dull red making a pattern in the black, cloudy sky above the Rollins' ranch.

Then Grandpa was running up the drive. "Martha! Jenny!" he cried. "Martha!"

Jeff couldn't remember leaving the car but he found himself running beside the old man. The crowd separated to let the man and boy through. It was then that Jeff realized the fire was not in the chinchilla unit at all, it was in the *house*. His chinchillas were not in danger but — where were Grandma and Jenny? His eyes searched for his grandmother and sister among the faces of the people who were their neighbors and friends.

He saw the firemen undoing the big black hose and getting to work. He was sure the whole house would be burned to the ground. He tried to think. Grandma Rollins wasn't feeling well so she and Jenny had stayed at home earlier that Sunday evening while Jeff and Grandpa had gone to church. Jeff had to practice his part for the coming Christmas program. Now, where were Grandma and Jenny?

"Over here, Clarence," the familiar voice of Bob Moor reached Jeff's ears above the noise of the neighbors, the sirens and the fire. Grandpa heard him too and turned toward a parked car.

The old rancher threw his arms around the blanket-clad figure of his wife, who was leaning against the car, supported there by Bob Moor.

"Oh, Martha, I'm so glad you're all right," he exclaimed with relief. "Jenny, where's Jenny?"

"I'm right here, Grandpa. I'm fine too," answered Jenny who stepped out from

"Isn't that some fire?" exclaimed Jeff's friend Tommy. "I never saw a house on fire before!"

behind Grandma.

Her brother grabbed her hand. "Boy, am I glad you're okay too," he said, a little embarrassed at himself. He hadn't noticed Tommy Moor until now.

Jeff's friend laid his hand on his shoulder and exclaimed, "Isn't that some fire? I guess I never saw a house on fire before!"

"Me neither," replied Jeff.

Grandma Rollins laid her head on her husband's shoulder and burst into tears as she tried to explain. "It was the tree, Clarence," she said tearfully. "I think the Christmas tree caught on fire first!"

Jeff could see Grandma's hands shaking. He wanted to help but he couldn't figure out anything to do, so he just stood there between Jenny and Tommy.

"We'd better take her to my house, Clarence," offered Mr. Moor.

Grandma objected weakly but Grandpa said firmly, "Now, Martha, you take Jenny and go to Bob's. I'll see to things here."

Grandpa always spoke kindly to his

family but Jeff was sure that he had never before heard him sound so tender.

"I'll drive you over, Mrs. Rollins," said a woman's voice.

Jeff was startled. It was the voice of Barbara Adams' mother. She seemed to have appeared out of nowhere. Jeff had never liked Barbara much and the twins had seen very little of her since Jenny was accused of cheating on a report which Barbara had done a few months ago. Now the girl's mother was offering them help! Grandma didn't argue further but left with Jenny and Mrs. Adams.

The smoke was no longer coming from the roof of the house. It looked as though the firemen had stopped the blaze.

Tommy grabbed Jeff's arm. "I think your Christmas tree and everything in the living room is burned up!" he said.

"So do I, Tommy," returned Jeff sadly. "We put all our packages under it this afternoon. All our Christmas presents are burned up."

Jeff looked up at Grandpa's white face. Tommy's father placed his strong arm across the old man's shoulders and helped him to the Moor's car.

"You'd better sit down, Clarence," he said. Then he opened the door and Grandpa sank into the front seat. His feet dangled loosely out the door.

"I'm sorry, Clarence." Mr. Moor stood close to Grandpa.

"How'd it start?" asked Grandpa.

"Martha said she thought there was some electrical problem," Mr. Moor explained. "She smelled it just before she saw the flame." He shook his head sadly. "It'll cost plenty, Clarence, but you're insured, aren't you?"

Grandpa nodded his head slowly. "Yes," he answered, "and I have so much for which to praise the Lord."

Mr. Moor looked at him quizzically and Jeff wondered what he meant. "You can talk about being thankful at a time like this?" asked Bob Moor.

"Yeah, what do you mean, Grandpa?" asked Jeff. "Grandma worked all year knitting and sewing for the whole family. And all her packages are gone now, as well as the front part of the house."

Grandpa pulled Jeff close to him. "Son," he began, "we have lost only things which can be replaced. Grandma, Jenny and the chinchillas weren't hurt a bit."

RESENTMENT

JEFF'S EYES popped open! The room seemed strange for a moment. Where was he? He turned his head. There was Tommy Moor in a sleeping bag lying on the floor next to him. Tommy's father was asleep in the bed at the other side of his son's room. Then Jeff remembered the fire! He was at Tommy's house because his grandparents' living room burned the night before, so Tommy and his father had taken them to the Moor's home.

The telephone was ringing. Tommy began to scramble out of his sleeping bag. "I'll get it, Dad," he offered sleepily.

Then they heard Grandma say, "Hello, this is the Moor residence, Mrs. Rollins speaking."

"Catch!" yelled Mr. Moor as he tossed his pillow at Tommy. "Martha already beat you to the phone." The pillow was coming Jeff's way. He caught it just in time. The whole room suddenly came alive. They squealed with laughter, as the boys and the man rolled and tumbled across the floor. When a knock at the door was heard they stopped only for a moment.

"Breakfast is ready," came Grandma's voice from the other side of the door.

"We'll be there in a minute, Grandma," Jeff called as Tommy tackled him one more time.

At the breakfast table Grandpa and Grandma looked pale and tired but happy as usual. Jenny ate quietly and did not join in the conversation.

"That was Mrs. Adams who called," Grandma said, sipping her coffee. "She is an interior decorator and, even though we hardly know her, she has organized some of our friends to come and help me clean up the house. She said she and the others would meet us there at seven o'clock. Because the children are on Christmas vacation she is bringing Barbara with her." She looked at the twins, then turned toward Tommy. "Since your father must go to work, Tommy," she said kindly, "you may come along too. There will be plenty to do for everybody."

As the car moved slowly up the Rollins' drive Jeff felt like crying. He reached for Jenny's hand and found it cold and trembling. What a mess! One end of the Rollins' ranch house was charred. Gray ashes lay everywhere. Here and there little wisps of smoke rose into the crisp air of the December morning.

The three young people crawled slowly

out of the car. "Sure was a scary fire, wasn't it?" Jenny asked as they stepped through the door. "Look at what's left of the Christmas tree and all the pretty packages that were under it!"

Jeff looked at the place where the living room had been. A shapeless mass of charred wood, half-covered with ashes, was all that was left of the lovely tree they had so recently decorated. The family moved slowly into the kitchen which had not burned but was covered with black soot.

"Hi, everybody!" Barbara came bounding into the room followed by her mother and several other neighbors who carried buckets, rags and other cleaning supplies.

Jeff thought Mrs. Adams acted as if she were a director, or as if the house were hers or something. He had never liked Barbara. It seemed to him that trouble always came to him and Jenny when she was around. Now the mother seemed worse than her daughter. He didn't like the way she told everybody what to do. He simply couldn't stand the way she pushed Grandma and Grandpa around in their own house. Resentment boiled inside of him. He knew he shouldn't feel that way but knowing didn't stop him. He wished Mrs. Adams hadn't decided to help!

"Okay, everybody, it looks as though there is smoke damage in every room. Here's what we will do," announced Mrs. Adams. "If we divide into teams and work together we can no doubt have everything but the living room back in order by tonight. It's only three days until Christmas and I am sure Mrs. Rollins wants things fixed before then."

She assigned each team to do a big job — washing walls, scrubbing floors or washing and ironing curtains and cleaning windows. She had written long lists of jobs on sheets of paper which she handed to each person with the command to, "Do these little detailed jobs if you have time."

No one seemed to mind being given a job but Jeff. He heard Grandma go so far as to say, "Grace Adams, I can't thank you enough for all you are doing!"

Grandpa took the boys outside to help with the chores and to check the chinchillas. Then they were to join the women and girls in the housecleaning.

It had been decided that the dining room would become the living room and the family would eat in the kitchen until a new living room could be built. Mrs. Adams was loaning them a couch which she had stored and several other neighbors were bringing in chairs, a lamp and some end tables. Each piece had to be vacuumed and polished before it could be put in its place. The furniture was placed on the patio where Jeff and Tommy began cleaning it.

As the boys worked, Grandma and Mrs. Adams who were cleaning closets and bedrooms, were hanging clothes on the line to air. Jeff and Tommy couldn't help but overhear their conversation.

"Martha, I have wanted to meet you and get to know you ever since Barbara and I

As Jeff and Tommy were busy cleaning the furniture, they couldn't help overhearing the women's conversation.

moved to Colorado," Mrs. Adams was saying. "It is a shame that I would put it off until trouble forced me to come to you."

Grandma sounded surprised. "Grace, I don't understand."

"Remember the trouble your granddaughter and my Barbara were in at school a few months ago?"

"Yes, of course," replied Grandma.

"Well," Mrs. Adams' voice sounded strange. "I'm a Christian—I know the Lord as my Saviour—but I haven't been faithful to Him. I haven't kept Barbara in Sunday School. When the teacher at school told me about how Jenny reacted to unfair accusations I knew you must be Christians." Mrs. Adams stopped working and placed her arm around Grandma's waist. "Martha, Barbara and I would like to begin attending your church. My daughter needs Jesus too."

Jeff gasped! His eyes were wide with amazement. He looked at Tommy who was staring at him in wonderment. Tommy found his tongue first. "She's not supposed to ask us to come to our church," he said. "We're supposed to ask her!"

Jeff sank into the chair he had been vacuuming. "You're right. We are supposed to ask her! And I should have asked Barbara to come to Sunday School a long time ago. I disliked her so much I think I didn't want her to come. Grandpa says that when you don't like somebody you ought to pray for them. I never prayed for Barbara or her mother. I never thought of it!"

Tommy set the can of furniture polish he had been using on the ground. "Let's go ask her to come next week to the Christmas program, Jeff," he said.

CHRISTMAS
SURPRISES

THE ROLLINS' HOUSE had been scrubbed and polished. In the dining room, which was now serving as a living room, stood a lovely Christmas tree with packages under it. Jeff was sitting cross-legged on the floor admiring the tree when his sister Jenny came in and plopped herself on the floor beside him.

"It's pretty but it's not the same," she commented softly.

"What do you mean?' asked Jeff.

"I mean this tree and the gifts under it are nice because our friends were so sweet about fixing it up for us but, well—" she shifted position. "You know what I mean, Jeff. We put the other tree up together, with Grandma and Grandpa. Then Grandpa read the Bible story about how God gave us His Son, Jesus, to die for our sins. He told us how the tree points people to Jesus, and how gifts remind us of God's Gift."

Jeff sighed. "It was nice," he said.

Jenny continued, "And the other gifts, the ones that burned, were all *made* for us by Grandma's own hands. She always makes us new sweaters. I guess it's like she says, she puts her love in the things she makes for us with each stitch. Then the things we had under the tree for them were made too. I had some hot pads for Grandma and a scarf for Grandpa. I know they both would have loved the leather book marks you made for their Bibles. Remember how much fun we had keeping the gifts a secret? This is not the same."

"Yeah, and we haven't heard from Mom and Dad, either. What do you suppose has happened to their letters lately?" Jeff gazed into the glowing lights of the tree.

Jenny answered in a voice that sounded far away. "You know how the mail is at Christmas time. We'll hear from them tomorrow—I hope."

Jeff's heart was heavy with loneliness as he climbed into his bed. It was Christmas Eve. He wondered if Jenny felt as unhappy as he did. They had never before been separated from their parents on Christmas!

He awoke several times in the night. Once he knelt by the window to look out. Snow was falling silently. He knew that tomorrow everything would be beautifully clothed in white fluff. He slipped back in the bed. But when his eyes opened again he felt strangely expectant. He heard voices— outside. He ran to the window.

"Jenny!" he screamed. "Jenny! Mom and Dad are here!" He was pulling on his jeans

with shaking hands. "Grandma! Grandpa! They're here!" He grabbed a T-shirt and pulled it on as he ran down the hall yelling, "Wake up everybody! Dad and Mom are here!"

His mother reached the front door just as he pulled it open. Jeff threw himself into her arms. "Mom, I love you!" he cried.

His father paid the taxi driver, picked up two suitcases and strode to the door. Jeff left his mother's arms as Jenny flew into them crying, "Oh Mommie, I'm so glad you're here!"

Mr. Rollins set down his suitcases and gathered his son into his arms. "Merry Christmas, Jeff! Merry Christmas!"

Grandpa and Grandma appeared in the doorway. Everyone was talking at once. Everyone was kissing everyone else. No one seemed to be listening until Grandpa shouted above the others, "Come inside, we'll all freeze out here in the snow!"

After a delightful breakfast the family gathered around the Christmas tree. Grandpa read the story of Jesus' birth from the second chapter of Luke. Then he prayed and it was time to open the gifts which had been waiting under the tree. The pile had grown considerably since Jeff and Jenny looked at them the night before. Each person in turn opened a gift while the others watched. When the contents of a box was disclosed there were "thank you's," "oh's" and "ah's."

Mr. and Mrs. Rollins had brought ski suits for Jeff and Jenny. When these boxes were opened the twins could hardly believe their eyes. Mr. Rollins promised, "I'll take you to Winter Park tomorrow and you both can begin to learn how to ski!"

Jeff felt he might burst with happiness and excitement. He remembered how unhappy he had been when his parents left last Fall. Suddenly, he turned to Grandpa and the words spilled out. "It really is God's will for kids to obey their parents, just like you said." Everyone laughed—including Jeff.

Finally, there were only two packages left

— one with Jenny's name and one with Jeff's.

"You open yours first," Jeff urged his sister.

Jenny ripped open the box. There was a soft, pink cloud! "Oh, it's lovely!" she exclaimed. "I have a new sweater after all!"

Jenny looked lovingly at her grandmother who said, "I didn't make it but the other one was just about like it."

Tears filled Jenny's eyes. She managed to say, "It's just beautiful, Grandma. Thank you!"

"Open yours, Jeff," urged his mother quietly.

Jeff looked at his package in puzzlement. It was the strangest looking package he had ever received. It was shaped like a flat book. On the inside he found a piece of Grandma's favorite stationery. He unfolded it and read:

"Dear Jeff,

Because you were so faithful in caring for them, Sparky and Matilda are alive and healthy. In this package you will

Jeff and Jenny had presents to open after all. As Jeff looked at the papers, he felt warm and glowy inside.

*find their records. They are valuable
animals — especially Sparky. He is a
clearer mutation than Blue Boy. Grandma and I want you to have all the profit
which we make from your chinchillas.
The money will probably pay for most
of your college education.*

Love,

Grandpa and Grandma."

Jeff stared at the papers. He didn't know what to say. Sparky and Matilda were worth a lot of money! He had never considered how much they were worth. He cared for them tenderly because he loved them! He felt warm and glowy inside.

Jenny broke the silence, "Jeff, that's wonderful!"

He looked from one of the old people to the other. "Thanks," he breathed.

His father leaned close to Grandpa, "It's hard to tell you how much this means to us, Dad," he said. "Now, Evelyn and I have a surprise for all of you."

The twins looked at their father. There

had been so many surprises that week, Jeff was not sure he could stand another one.

There was a twinkle in his father's eyes. Mr. Rollins turned to Grandma and Grandpa as he spoke.

"Evelyn is feeling so much better now than she did when we left for Alaska last Fall that I have accepted a transfer from the bush station where I have been working to go to Anchorage. We have surely missed the twins and we appreciate your willingness to care for them. We can stay with you for a week and then we will be taking Jeff and Jenny with us."

There was absolute silence in the warm room which smelled of pine. Everyone seemed stunned. Then Jeff almost screamed, "Dad, you mean Jenny and I are going to ALASKA?"

WITNESSES

JEFF ROLLINS swallowed hard. But it didn't help. The lump in his throat seemed to get larger. He hadn't realized how hard it would be to leave Grandpa and Grandma Rollins, his best friend Tommy and Mrs. Penny, the cocker spaniel.

Jenny pulled on his sleeve. "Jeff," his sister said softly, "I sure didn't know leaving the chinchilla ranch would be like this!" Her voice quivered.

Jeff kept his face turned toward the window of the huge jet plane. He didn't want her to see the tears that filled his eyes. That whole Fall in Colorado he and Jenny had longed to join their mother and astronaut father in Alaska. Now they were sitting across the aisle from their parents. The plane began to move forward. They were on their way to Anchorage!

Jeff looked back, hoping to see his loved ones one more time. There they were—still waving! His hands tightened around the New Testament Grandpa had given him as they parted. He had seen Jenny stuff hers into her purse, but he felt like hanging on to his.

As the plane ascended and began to bank he looked at the land below. Then he thought he saw the Rollins ranch for a moment! He was not only leaving his friends and the old couple he loved most next to his own parents but he was leaving Sparky and Matilda—his very own chinchillas! The tears would not be held back any longer. They streamed down his face and dropped on the black leather of the Testament in his lap.

"You are the Astronaut Rollins' twins, aren't you?" a smiling stewardess asked. She looked neat and friendly as she slid into the empty seat next to Jenny. "Your names are Jeffery and Jennifer."

Jenny sighed and tried to smile. "Everybody calls us Jeff and Jenny," she explained. But Jeff didn't raise his head.

"I read about your father's work in the paper," the cheery voice continued. "You two are lucky to have such a wonderful father. But you look as though you have lost your last friend! Things surely aren't as bad as that. You are headed for Alaska. Isn't that about the most wonderful thing that ever happened to you?"

Jeff intently studied the lovely face of the young lady. "It *is* wonderful to go to Alaska," he began. "But I don't think it's the *most* wonderful thing that has happened to me. How about you Jenny?"

His sister shook her head. "The best thing that ever happened to me was the night I was saved," she answered firmly.

The stewardess's eyes sparkled with interest. "You kids seem to have led exciting lives. What were you saved from, Jenny?"

There was a look of happiness in Jenny's eyes. "Sin. I was saved from sin."

The stewardess flinched as though someone had suddenly stuck a pin in her finger. The smile faded from her face and her eyes seemed to turn to stone. But Jeff did not notice. He was thoughtful. "There isn't anything more important or exciting than trusting Jesus to save you from sin," he said. "That is the most exciting thing that ever happened to me, too."

A strange look came into the eyes of the stewardess. "My roommate is religious," she remarked as if to herself. "She says things like you do. She's always trying to tell me I need to be saved from sin, too. Maybe she's right. You kids seem to think it's important."

"Oh, it is!" Jenny agreed emphatically.

"I went to Vacation Bible School when I was a little girl," the young woman informed them. Then she added with more emphasis, "And I was baptized when I was in high school. I'm not as bad as you seem to think."

Jeff scooted forward in his seat. "But have you ever trusted Jesus to save you and wash your sins away? You see, to get saved you have to *know* Jesus—in your heart I mean."

The stewardess's eyes were puzzled. Jeff knew she was not taking him seriously. "I don't quite get you, Jeff," she said. "But you feel better now, don't you?"

Jeff knew this young woman needed Jesus, because everybody does. He also knew that she didn't want to talk about it anymore, but he made one more attempt to help her. "My dad could tell you better than Jenny and I."

"I *don't* want to talk about it to your dad," came the quick answer.

Jeff handed his New Testa-
ment to the pretty stewardess.
She promised she would read in
it about how to be saved.

But Jeff did not give up. "Would you read about how to get saved?" he asked.

She relaxed again and smiled at the boy. "If you think it's that important I'll read about it sometime," she promised.

Jeff held out the Testament Grandpa Rollins had given him a few hours before. "Would you read this?"

The young woman hesitated. "Well, I promised I'd read about it. Since you are so persistent . . ." Her lovely smile returned. "I'll read your book, Jeff, but give me your address so I can return it to you."

They arrived in Anchorage that afternoon. It was hard to believe.

Inside their new apartment, Jeff felt strange. He set his suitcase on the bed and collapsed next to it. The doorbell was ringing! Jeff ran to answer it.

"Special delivery for Mr. Christopher Rollins." The uniformed postman smiled.

"Dad! Mom! Jenny!" Jeff yelled. They all ran to join him.

Mr. Rollins tore open the envelope. "It's

from the Welches!"

"You mean Uncle Keith and Aunt Lorraine?" questioned Jenny. "They're working at a mission station in Chile, aren't they, Daddy?"

"Is something wrong, Chris?" questioned Mrs. Rollins.

"No, no. It seems that your nephew will be joining us soon to attend school here in the States. They have been trying to contact us for several days because Rick is already on his way."

"That's wonderful, Daddy!" squealed Jenny.

"Yeah, it is!" agreed Jeff. "Rick always was a lot of fun, even if he is lots older than us."

"Wonderful?" questioned the twins' father. "Yes, I guess it will be fun to have another boy in our family."

TROUBLE MULTIPLIES

SURE ENOUGH, Rickey Welch turned out to be as much fun as Jeff and Jenny had remembered. They had not seen him for five years. They were tiny little kids then and Rickey had been of junior age. Now he was in his junior year of high school.

"Rick, do you think I could really go with you to Dan's house to see his father's ham radio equipment?" Jeff's eyes sparkled with excitement. "Maybe Mr. Bradley will let me talk to somebody or work one of the radios."

"Sure, Astro, you can go with me," replied Jeff's cousin. "Mr. Bradley likes kids—especially kids that are interested in his hobby. Dan and I are going to work on his car Saturday. It needs a new transmission. You get your chores done around here and you can go too."

Saturday morning Jeff worked diligently helping Rickey clean the room the boys shared. As soon as they finished both boys hurried to the kitchen table. Rickey grabbed a metal file box marked *Saturday Chores* and opened it, holding it toward Jeff.

"You first, Astro," he said.

Jeff pulled out a piece of folded paper and read the two words his mother had written, "Wash windows." "That's easy, what's yours?"

" 'Vacuum and dust living room,' " Rickey read slowly. "I'll have my job done in no time. Will you be ready to go in an hour?" Rickey was already pulling the sweeper out of its place in the closet.

The boys had decided to take a bus to the Bradley home but when they told Mr. Rollins about their plans he offered to let Rickey take the car. On the way Jeff and Rickey chattered about installing the transmission in Dan's car and Mr. Bradley's work with the Civil Air Patrol. Dan's father headed the Alaskan Air Patrol. It was his job to pick up distress calls and to send help. When people got lost the C.A.P. helped to find them. When storms hit the Anchorage area the Patrol often searched for missing planes.

Mr. Bradley was an older man, retired from his government job. Now he did air rescue work. He explained his fascinating equipment and let Jeff talk on a routine call.

It was late when Rickey and Dan finished their work on Dan's car. Mrs. Bradley invited the boys, her husband and Jeff to the kitchen for cake. When they had finished eating, Dan pulled out his cigarettes and offered Rickey one. Jeff almost fell off his chair when Rickey said, "Thanks, Dan," and casually lit up.

All the way home Jeff sat quietly looking out the window and thinking. He knew that a Christian's body is the home of the Holy Spirit. Therefore, a Christian should never do anything to hurt his body. He also knew that smoking could destroy the body by causing cancer and other diseases. Rickey was a Christian—at least Jeff thought he was!

"Hey, Astro, let's go in the house." Rickey's words startled Jeff. The car was already parked! He hadn't noticed that they were home.

Mr. Rollins met them at the door with an anxious look. "Rick, you have company." He sounded so strange Jeff wondered if he had a cold or something. "His name is Captain Murphy. He's in the living room," Jeff's father informed them.

The boy watched his father and Rickey disappear into the living room. He was still standing in the hall when Jenny appeared in the kitchen doorway. "Come here, Jeff," she whispered.

Mrs. Rollins was sitting at the kitchen table with an open receipt book, but she wasn't looking at it. The twins pulled chairs close on either side of her and sat down. Jenny couldn't keep quiet any longer. Her eyes were wide and worried.

"Jeff," she blurted, "that's a policeman who wants to see Rickey. He thinks Rick stole some car parts. The parts were in the top of your closet!"

Jeff felt as though he had been socked in the stomach.

"Did you know they were there, son?" Mrs. Rollins cupped her hand over Jeff's on the table.

Jeff stared at his mother. "No, Mom, honest, I didn't know." His words tumbled one over the other. "I don't think Rick is a Christian, Mom. He smokes! I saw him today. And now maybe he stole something." Jeff laid his head on his arms. Sobs shook his body.

Mrs. Rollins put her arm across his

Jeff suddenly felt sick. He put his head down on the table while his mother tried to comfort him.

shoulders while Jenny wiped tears from her own cheeks.

"Your father and I were aware of the smoking, Jeff," his mother said softly. "But we can't know if Rickey is saved or not. We must pray for him."

Captain Murphy's investigation revealed that the car parts *were* stolen but that Dan and Rickey had bought them from another boy. Both boys were cleared. It was a relief to know that Rickey was not involved in the theft, but Jeff knew his whole family was concerned over Rickey's spiritual condition.

That evening Rickey brought in the newspaper. The headlines screamed at him! There had been an extensive flood near Concepcion, Chile, Rickey turned white and shouted, "Uncle Chris! My Mom and Dad are only about forty miles from there!"

Taking the paper from the boy's shaking hand, Mr. Rollins replied quietly, "We'd better read the details before we get so excited."

The details caused Mr. Rollins and Rickey

to sit by the phone for hours trying to get a call through to Chile. But they were unable to contact the Welches. Rickey became more and more distressed.

Finally he said, "Uncle Chris, maybe Mr. Bradley could find out about them on the short wave radio."

The two anxious families waited tensely while Mr. Bradley contacted a ham operator in Chile. He was finally able to talk to a young Chilean who had worked for the Welches. Rickey and the boy spoke in rapid Spanish.

Then Rickey turned from the microphone to Mr. Rollins. His face was gray and he spoke through tightly clenched teeth. "They're missing!" His voice rose to a hysterical pitch. "Uncle Chris, they didn't have to die. It happened because they stayed in that dirty old mission!"

Mr. Rollins spoke slowly as though he were weighing each word before he said it. "Rick, you know that souls are dying in Chile without Christ. Those people need the

Saviour as you and I need Him. Your parents did what they felt was the Lord's will for them. And don't forget, they may still be alive. I'm sure they would want you to put your trust in Christ too."

Rickey seemed to gain control of his emotions. He looked at his uncle and then at the others who were listening silently.

"I know all that talk about salvation, assurance, faith—the works," he said slowly and with emphasis, "and I don't want to hear it anymore—*not ever!*"

HER NAME
WAS EVA

"HAVE YOU ever tried to ski before, Rick?" Jenny asked while she sat in the back of the station wagon between her brother and Rickey.

"Never been on them in my life." Rickey grinned at her.

"It's fun, Rick," Jeff joined the conversation, "even if I do spend half my time trying to untangle my feet."

"Alyeska Ski Resort—coming up!" Mr.

Rollins called from the driver's seat.

Mr. Rollins drove the car to the parking lot and into a space between a little Volkswagen and a bus. Everyone piled out and headed toward the buildings where the twins and Rickey rented equipment. Mr. and Mrs. Rollins, who were experienced skiers, had their own things.

When everyone was ready they labored to the beginner's slope. Rickey stood at the bottom and gazed up. Dark figures zigzagged down the hill.

"That's the *beginner's* slope?" he exclaimed.

"Sure, come on, Rick," Jenny laughed, but she remembered the empty feeling she had the first time she looked at a beginner's slope.

Rickey spent the rest of the morning laboring up the slope then trying to snowplow down. The twins stayed close by him laughing uproariously when one of them floundered into the powdery white drifts. Mr. and Mrs. Rollins gave helpful pointers to the young people and laughed with them.

The four were standing at the bottom of the hill watching Rickey come down. Before Jenny knew what was happening Rickey was stuck, with his feet going in opposite directions.

"How did you do that?" called Mr. Rollins as he moved, laughing, to Rickey's rescue.

"It's a neat trick—don't you agree, Uncle Chris?" Rickey shouted. They all laughed at his good-natured attitude.

"I'm starving!" Jenny announced. "Let's go eat lunch."

They were entering the cafeteria when a familiar voice called, "Hey, Rick, I didn't know you were coming up here!" The voice belonged to Rickey's friend, Dan Bradley.

Jenny was persistent. "I'm gonna get in line, I want to eat!" She and Jeff moved to the end of the line ahead of a group of older ladies. The rest of the family were still talking.

Suddenly two young couples stumbled

across the room from the doorway. They were laughing boisterously and hanging on one another. The blonde woman sauntered over to the twins standing in line.

"You kids get out of here!" she ordered. "Did you hear me?" She turned to her companion. "I don't like pesky kids. They shouldn't be allowed out of their cages."

Jenny reached for Jeff's hand. She found him tense but he said nothing to the insulting woman.

The man with her snickered but said, "Come on, Eva, leave those kids alone."

"I will not," she said loudly. "I want in that line and those kids are in my way." With this, Eva shoved Jenny so hard she felt her full weight land on Jeff's foot.

"I'm sorry, Jeff." Jenny was near tears.

"It's okay, Jenny. Let them get in line in front of you."

Jenny was surprised at her brother but she stood as close to him as she could in order to allow room for the couple. Suddenly she realized her father had come across the room to them.

"You kids having trouble?" he asked.

Before Jenny could answer, Jeff said, "No, no, Dad, everything's fine now."

When the family and Dan were seated at a table Jeff explained what had happened. He whispered, "That man has a *gun* inside his jacket. I saw it. That's why I told you we were okay, Dad."

After a few minutes the incident was forgotten. They enjoyed their lunch.

Dan and Rickey were learners so they decided to spend the afternoon on the beginner's slope together. Mr. and Mrs. Rollins moved to the expert slopes and the twins were soon on their way up the mountain to the slope they had chosen, sitting side by side on the chair lift.

"It will take us a long time to ski down this slope, Jeff," said Jenny. "Did you bring one of those maps of the runs so we won't get lost?"

"Yeah, here it is."

The two scooted off the lift and opened the

map. They decided on a route and started in a direction that appeared to be deserted. However, the snow still showed tracks of recent skiers. They laughed and fell in the snow, scrambled back to their feet and tried again and again.

"Look!" Jenny stopped so fast she nearly fell over. Jeff caught up with her.

"What's the matter?" he asked, looking down the slope in the direction Jenny's mittened hand pointed. His eyes found a black heap of cloth lying in the snow. He also saw a semicircle of deep red. "Somebody's hurt!" he cried.

The twins maneuvered themselves to the spot. Jenny snapped off her skis and bent over the unconscious body. She pushed back the blonde hair and gasped! "Jeff, it's Eva— that lady in the cafeteria! She's hurt awfully bad. What will we do!"

Jeff stared at the unconscious, crumpled body for a moment. "She must have hit that rock. With that great big cut on her arm she might bleed to death before we can get help.

Jenny was startled as a ski patrolman told her, "If she lives, she will owe her life to you and your brother."

Jenny, fold your scarf and press it down hard on her cut. Stay with her and I'll go get the Ski Patrol."

Jenny sat in the snow beside the quiet form and watched her brother snowplow as fast as possible down the mountain and out of sight. Her eyes turned to the white face and she began to pray. "Dear Lord, I don't think this lady knows about You, so, if it's Your will, please don't let her die. And, when she wakes up send somebody to tell her about You. Amen."

Jenny sat patiently beside the injured woman, stirring from time to time to help keep herself warm. Finally, the hum of a motor reached her and soon the men of the Ski Patrol had the woman bundled onto a stretcher and placed snugly on the Skidoo. As they started down the mountain with the woman, one ski patrolman turned to Jenny and said, "If she lives, she will owe her life to you and your brother. It could have been hours before we found her clear over here."

In the car on the way home the twins took

turns relating their exciting experience to their parents and Rickey. Jenny finished by saying, "I sure do hope Eva lives and finds Jesus as her Saviour. I think she needs Him."

Her shocked cousin shouted, *"Eva!* But that's the gal who was so rude to you kids in the cafeteria. Why did you even bother with her? I'll bet she's wanted by the FBI or something!"

AT
THE FUR
RENDEZVOUS

"HERE THEY COME, Rick, look!" Jeff bubbled with excitement.

"Do twirlers always lead parades?" Jenny asked.

"I think so. Haven't you kids ever been to a parade before?" Rickey sounded amused.

"Yes, but I can't remember much about it." Jeff's heart seemed to pound so hard he wondered if the people around him could hear it too. But he couldn't help feeling the spirit of the people who had come to see the Fur Rendezvous parade, join the Sled Dog races, watch the Eskimo dances and observe the exhibitions and art show. The twins and Rickey had only come for Saturday afternoon though the February Rendezvous lasted ten days.

Jeff imagined what it would have been like to be a Christian fur trapper. He thought of how he might have brought in several hundred dollars worth of furs to sell at a rendezvous. He wondered if he would have the courage to tell other trappers of his Saviour. He knew that the mountain men who did this work were often rough and rowdy.

But the spell of his dream was broken when Rickey grabbed his arm and began to move with the crowd to the exhibition hall. The parade was over. "That was interesting!" Jeff exclaimed loudly to his sister and Rickey.

The three ran up the steps of the building which housed the art exhibits and moved to the first painting. Jenny was quite far ahead of the boys when a well-dressed man sauntered up to them. He carried his suit coat. His tie was loose and hung to one side. Jeff noticed that his shirt collar was unbuttoned. The man's hair was steel gray and his eyes matched it. He flung his arm across Rickey's shoulders and put his face close to the boy's. Jeff was on the other side but even from that distance he couldn't help but smell the liquor on the man's breath.

"Young man, I want to give you something." He slurred the words together until Jeff could hardly understand him. "Don't tell anybody." Then he thrust a roll of paper into Rickey's coat pocket. Before the startled boys could say a word he disappeared into the crowded street.

"What'd he give you, Rick?" Jeff's eyes were wide with curiosity. Rickey reached into his pocket and pulled out a roll of ten dollar bills!

"Wow!" he breathed.

"You said it!" Jeff was appalled. "I never

saw so much money in my whole life! Wow! What are you going to do with it?"

Rickey stuffed the roll of bills into his inner pocket and buttoned his coat. "I don't know, Astro, but let's keep this between you and me. Don't tell anybody else."

That night after the boys had gone to bed Jeff called softly, "Rick, what are ya gonna do with all that money that man gave you?"

There was a long pause, then Rickey answered, "I'm going to *spend* that five hundred dollars. That's what I'm going to do with it."

"But Rick, it's not yours!"

"No? Then who does it belong to? He gave it to me, didn't he? I don't even know the guy's name. Now, how do you suppose I'm going to return it to someone whose name I don't know?"

Jeff hadn't thought of that but he insisted, "I think you ought to tell Dad about it then."

"Why should I?"

"Well, why shouldn't you? If the money is

really yours, Dad won't take it from you. I don't think you honestly think it's yours either. That's why you are keeping it a secret from Dad."

Suddenly, two strong hands closed like steel around Jeff's arms and he found himself sitting bolt upright facing Rickey in the darkness.

"Listen, Astro, you keep still and mind your own business. I mean it." Rickey's voice was threatening. "I intend to have a motorcycle with that money and no one is going to stop me, ya hear?"

A few days later Rickey came home with a motorcycle. When Mr. Rollins questioned him about paying for it he told his uncle he had used his savings for a down payment and would pay the rest from the money he received working at a part-time job. Jeff thought his father seemed doubtful and the younger boy looked miserable, but he remained silent.

Several weeks later, a man came home to dinner with Mr. Rollins. The boys were busy doing their homework when the men arrived. They had just finished when Jenny came to call them. They hurried to the living room.

Jeff's face turned white and his mouth fell open as he stared at the man before him. Rickey, too, appeared astonished! Mr. Crammer's gray eyes matched his steel gray hair!

"Rick, that's h-h-him," Jeff stuttered. "He's the man that gave you the money."

"Why are you acting so shocked, boys?" asked Mr. Rollins.

When the boys told the story of the past weeks, Mr. Crammer's face turned scarlet. He said to Mr. Rollins. "Chris, I am as guilty in all this as the boys. The five hundred dollars belongs to the government. I was supposed to use it for expenses to get back to California. Instead, I cashed the check, but I couldn't remember what I had done with the money. I was going to tell you a sob story to try to borrow it from you tonight."

Rickey tried to take the motorcycle back to

Jeff could see that Mr. Crammer was embarrassed. Would he admit that he had done such a foolish thing?

the store, but he found the proprietor completely uncooperative. He sold it for only part of the amount he had paid for it. He faced paying back the balance of the five hundred dollars in payments.

The day he gave his last payment to his uncle the family was at the dinner table.

"I hope this experience has taught you boys that we must be genuinely honest and straightforward all the time," said Mr. Rollins. "If you had told me about the money sooner maybe we would have avoided so much trouble."

"We know now, Dad," Jeff assured him.

"We sure do," agreed Rickey. Then he changed the subject. "How would you kids like to drive out to William's Hill and go sledding tomorrow?"

"That would be wonderful, Rick!" chorused Jeff and Jenny.

JENNY AND THE ICE TRAP

"EVERYBODY ready?" Rickey called, standing at the front door of the Rollins' apartment. "I'm going to load the toboggan on the station wagon. Then I'm pulling out to pick up Greta."

Jenny's head popped through her doorway. She was dressed for sledding and was pulling on her mittens. "You're picking up Cara Lee's sister?" she questioned. "How come she's going to William's Hill with *us*?"

"Because I asked her to go with us!" Rickey gave Jenny's stocking cap a quick tweak and ran out the door.

Jenny followed him chanting, "Rick has a girl, Rick has a girl."

Jeff burst through the front doorway. "Hey, wait for me. Gordon is going with us. We have to pick him up too. What's this I hear about your love life, Rick?"

After Rickey secured the toboggan on top of the car the three young people piled in and Rickey started the motor. "Okay, you two, knock it off. Greta is a sharp gal. And I sorta like her. So, none of your wisecracks."

Rickey picked up Jeff's friend, Gordon Lucas. Then he drove to the Mason home where Cara Lee and her sister joined the happy group. Rickey opened his door to let Greta slide in next to him. Finally they were winding toward the foot of William's Hill. It was a good wide slope and made a long run from the top, clear across Blue Creek at the bottom, to an area of level snow.

Rickey stopped the car. The young people

in warm sweaters and wool stocking caps helped him unload the toboggan. They began the climb to the top of the hill. "We'll take it easy the first time down," Rickey explained. "This toboggan will hold only four of us so we'll have to take turns."

Jeff turned a happy face toward his cousin. "I think you should guide it every time, Rick, and Greta should go with you every time. How about Jenny and Cara Lee taking turns with Gordon and me every other time?"

Everyone agreed that this was a wise and fair arrangement.

They gathered about the toboggan at the top of the hill. Rickey took his place in the front while Jeff and Gordon helped to hold it long enough for the girls to get on board. Jenny quickly found herself flying over the white expanse of snow, holding tight and gulping to catch her breath in the crisp afternoon air.

Again and again the toboggan was pulled laboriously up the hill, and descended with its load of bright young people who laughed and chattered merrily. Each time they flew over the little creek at the bottom of the ravine, and slowed safely to a stop on the level snow beyond.

Finally, Rickey, who had been doing most of the work pulling the toboggan up the hill, sat down in the snow. "I'm beat," he said. "I can't pull that thing up the hill another time."

"But, Rick," objected Jenny, "I want to guide it down one time."

Her young cousin looked at her sharply. "Are you sure you can handle it?" he asked.

"Sure I can!" Jenny was positive. "If you guys are afraid to ride with me, Cara Lee and I will come down by ourselves."

Cara Lee didn't seem to share Jenny's daring. "We will?" she asked.

Gordon was starting up the hill pulling the toboggan. "Let's see you guide it, Jenny," he challenged. "I'll ride with you."

When they reached the top of William's Hill, Jenny took her place in front and Cara

Lee scooted in behind her. Gordon and Jeff settled themselves behind the girls. Rickey and Greta had remained seated in the snow at the bottom of the slope — watching.

The toboggan started to move, slowly at first—then faster and faster! Jenny tried to lean one way and then the other as Rickey had done to keep it in the well-traveled path, but somehow it was different when *she* was in the driver's seat. Suddenly, a huge bank of drifted snow arose before them.

"Look out!" she screamed.

The toboggan turned over, scattering young people across the snow just beyond the creek. They rolled like balls in the powdery cold and came up scared but unharmed. That is, all except Jenny!

As the toboggan bumped across Blue Creek, she was thrown into the air. The creek was frozen, but a spring running between the snow and alternate layers of water and ice had formed a hidden pool of water which was covered with thin ice. Jenny broke through the ice at this spot.

As the togobban bumped across the creek, Jenny was thrown into the air and broke through the thin ice of a hidden pool.

Jenny, are you okay?" yelled Rickey running across the snow with Greta at his heels. He was pulling off his sweater as he ran. He dropped it at the side of the creek, where Greta stopped.

"Oh, Rick, she's hurt!" cried Greta. "Look at the blood on her forehead—and it's running down her cheek!"

Rickey fell on his knees and reached under Jenny's arms. He managed to stay on solid ground himself and pulled her to safety.

Jenny's teeth chattered like a machine gun. She had never felt so cold in all her life. Not only her teeth chattered but she shook all over. She saw the other kids in a circle looking down at her, but everything began to spin and she couldn't hear them anymore. Then it seemed from somewhere far away she heard a piercing scream! It was Cara Lee!

"She's dead! She's dead! I know she is!" screamed the girl.

Jeff came running from the car with a

blanket. Rickey and Greta quickly wrapped Jenny in it. Then Greta turned to her sister, "Cara Lee, stop that screaming this instant." But Cara Lee didn't seem to hear her. She continued to scream hysterically, "She's dead! She's dead!"

Greta grabbed her little sister and shook her while the others watched in astonishment.

"Stop it! Stop it!" she demanded. "I don't want to do this, Cara Lee." The older girl slapped Cara Lee across the face! The shock calmed the younger girl but she sobbed continually all the way back.

At the apartment, Greta helped Mrs. Rollins get Jenny into a warm bed. They washed the ugly cut on her face while Rickey called the doctor.

When things were back to normal and Jenny had eaten some hot soup, Greta turned to Cara Lee. "Honey," she began, "I'm sorry I had to slap you. I know it isn't easy to be calm when there is an accident like Jenny's, but your hysterics made me leave Jenny when she needed attention. I had to stop your hysterics."

Cara Lee didn't answer. She looked at the floor and twisted her hands nervously.

"Oh, Greta," protested Jenny weakly. "Don't blame Cara Lee. She's my best friend and she loves me."

LOSING A GIFT

JENNY was restless. She had missed school since she fell in the creek because her legs were still wobbly. Dr. Mills said that was a result of the shock. But on this Saturday she felt fine. She had cleaned her room and took a short nap. She moved nonchalantly to the piano. After practicing for fifteen or twenty minutes she picked up a magazine from her mother's rack. There would surely be something to read.

But the magazine wasn't interesting. She tossed it back into the rack and slouched in her father's favorite chair. Jeff and Rickey had gone to a basketball game. She decided to see if she could help her mother who was busy in the kitchen. As she was getting up, Mr. Rollins appeared in the doorway.

"Miss Priss," he said, "I've been looking for you. I hear you need a new pair of shoes. How about taking a shopping trip with your Dad?"

Jenny flew across the room to her father. "Daddy, I'd love it," she squealed.

"Can you be ready in thirty minutes?"

"I sure can." She ran to her room, slipped off her jeans and sweater and pulled on her blue knit suit. It was her father's favorite and she wanted to please him. She grabbed the brush, smoothed her hair and put on a blue band.

As they were leaving, Mr. Rollins called, "We'll be back for dinner."

"Make sure you're on time!" Her mother came to the kitchen door for a moment.

Jenny loved to shop and her father knew she did. They looked in several stores before she found the pair of shoes she wanted. They were green patent leather slippers. When she made her selection Mr. Rollins looked doubtful. "Can you wear green shoes with all of your clothes?" he asked.

She hadn't thought of how the shoes would look with her dresses! "I guess not, Daddy," she answered with disappointment. "Maybe I'd better take the brown ones."

After the shoes were paid for and under Mr. Rollins' arm, he turned to Jenny and said. "How about a Coke?" They stopped at a drugstore and Jenny chattered continually. She told him about the kids at Sunday School and how much fun she had practicing her part for the Easter pageant which the Juniors were to present on Easter Sunday. Soon it was time to go home.

They were coming around the last corner when Jenny exclaimed, "Daddy, there's Jeff and Rick!" Rickey was parking the little

Volkswagen as Mr. Rollins pulled in behind the boys.

Mrs. Rollins met them at the door. Jenny thought she seemed nervous. She noticed that her mother was wearing one of her best dresses.

"Dinner is on the table, so come to the dining room," Mrs. Rollins announced.

Jeff and Jenny stepped to the doorway almost together. "It's dark in there, Mom. I'll turn on the li . . ." Jeff didn't finish his sentence.

"SURPRISE!!!"

Their delighted friends were already seated around the table singing, "Happy Birthday!"

"But our birthday's not 'til tomorrow!" Jenny explained to Cara Lee as she slipped into her place beside her friend.

"Tomorrow's Sunday," Cara Lee reminded her. "This way we knew you'd both be surprised."

The birthday dinner was delicious. There was Jenny's favorite meat—pork chops. But their mother hadn't forgotten Jeff either. On another platter were meat balls smothered in mushroom gravy. Jenny ate her salad, vegetables and pickles without realizing it— she was so happy. She looked over at her brother. He seemed to be having a good time too— at *their* birthday party. Dessert included two cakes—a pink one for Jenny and a chocolate one for Jeff. Each guest had a piece of each.

After dinner they played games. It was time to open the packages which were piled high in one corner of the living room. The twins took turns opening the lovely gifts one at a time. Jenny had one more left. She read the card which was signed, "With my love, Daddy." She wondered what could be in it. When the top was lifted, there they were— the green slippers! "Oh, Daddy, you bought them, but how?"

Mr. Rollins laughed and said, "It wasn't easy."

The last guest was leaving when the phone rang. Jenny answered. It was long

The operator told her it was a Mr. Rollins in Denver. He wanted to speak to Jeff or Jenny Rollins. "I'm Jenny!" she said.

distance from Denver. The operator said Clarence Rollins wanted to talk to Jeff or Jenny Rollins. "I'm Jenny and that's my grandpa."

Jenny was overcome with excitement. "Oh, Grandpa is it really you? It's so good to talk to you! But why did you call? Are you and Grandma okay?"

"We're fine, Jenny." The sound of Grandpa's voice made her homesick for the chinchilla ranch. "We called to tell you and Jeff 'Happy Birthday' and to find out why you didn't let us know how you like the puppy."

Jenny nearly dropped the receiver. *"Puppy!* What puppy?" she asked.

Grandpa, explained that Mrs. Penny, his cocker spaniel, had puppies and he and Grandma had sent the twins the cutest one.

"But Grandpa, we didn't get it! When should it have been here?" questioned Jenny.

"The day before yesterday!" came the appalling answer.

"Oh, no!" was all Jenny could say because the tears were beginning to trickle down her face and a big lump was stuck in her throat. One of *Mrs. Penny's* puppies was lost!

Her father took the phone and discussed the matter with Grandpa Rollins while Jenny tearfully told the rest of the family about the missing puppy. She said, "Jeff, Grandpa's puppy, I mean, Mrs. Penny's puppy . . . no, no, I mean *our* puppy is lost!"

When Mr. Rollins returned from the phone he looked concerned. "Dad sent the pup last Wednesday. It should have arrived in our airport Thursday. I can't imagine what could have happened to it. We know it got as far as Vancouver. I'll be flying there Monday on business. Dad was sure the pup got that far. So, Jeff, you can go with me and we will see if we can find it—okay?"

"Okay, Dad!"

MIDNIGHT IS DAVID'S DOG

JEFF ROLLINS once more found himself looking out the window of a plane. This one was not as large as the one that brought him to Anchorage, but Jeff didn't seem to notice. He was thinking of the lost puppy that Grandpa and Grandma Rollins had sent. Wasn't it great — one of Mrs. Penny's puppies for their birthday! But it had not arrived! Grandpa had traced it as far as Vancouver, British Columbia, but had not located the little dog. Jeff scooted down in his seat and sighed. He was glad his father had asked him to go with him on this business trip to the Canadian city, so they could try to locate the puppy.

He felt as though he had eaten rocks for breakfast. "Could the puppy still be alive?" he wondered. Grandpa had put it on the plane almost a week ago! Jeff knew the airlines transported animals in small cages. If someone did not care for the baby dog it was probably *dead!* Jeff gasped involuntarily.

"Good morning, Mr. Rollins." The cheery voice of the stewardess brought Jeff out of his thoughts. His father greeted her politely. "You must be Jeff," she said, turning to the boy.

Jeff tried to smile and answered with a friendly, "Hello."

"I have something for you, young man," she continued. "I'll get it and be back in a second." She moved quickly away. Jeff and his father exchanged a puzzled look.

When she returned the stewardess looked as though she had been crying but she smiled at Jeff. "You flew to Alaska a few months ago, didn't you?" she began. Jeff nodded. "While you were on the plane did you give this to the stewardess?"

Jeff's eyes widened. She was holding the New Testament that Grandpa Rollins had given him. "Yes, I did," he answered taking the book from her hand.

"The stewardess you gave it to was my roommate, Pat," she explained.

Jeff remembered well the young woman he had tried to lead to the Lord. "She promised she'd read my Testament — did she?" he asked eagerly.

"She sure did, Jeff." Tears filled the eyes of the stewardess but she went on. "Let me tell you about it. I was going to return your Testament by mail but when I saw your name on my passenger list I wanted to tell you personally. Pat told me how she promised you she would read about salvation. I encouraged her to begin with the Gospel of

John. She began asking me questions about how to be saved and one night I was able to lead her to make a decision to trust Jesus. The next day we were both scheduled to make a flight to Texas, but I was sick so she went alone. The plane went down and..." The girl's voice broke. Jeff could hardly hear her say, "Pat was killed!"

Mr. Rollins spoke softly to the stewardess and Jeff tried to look out the window again. He breathed a little prayer. "Oh, thank You, Heavenly Father," he said. "Thank you for letting me help Pat find You before she died. Amen."

Jeff waited impatiently while his father took care of his business, then they began the search for the missing puppy. Mr. Rollins talked to a clerk who sent him to another clerk. Jeff and his father had waited in so many lines and talked to so many clerks he was beginning to think they would never find the puppy.

At lunch time he sat across from Mr. Rollins in the terminal cafeteria and asked desperately, "Dad, what are we going to do? We don't know any more about the puppy than when we came."

"Mr. Rollins, I understand you're looking for a lost dog." The voice startled Jeff so that he nearly choked on his milk. When he looked up he saw that the voice belonged to a janitor.

"What do you know about the lost pup?" asked Mr. Rollins eagerly.

"Well, about a week ago," the man explained, "I heard the baggage clerks arguing about this pup. It seems it arrived here without a tag and no one could decide what to do with the little thing. So I took him over to Victoria to my nephew, David. Today, I overheard you talking to the desk clerk. I imagine that little cocker is your dog all right."

The thrill of finding the puppy made Jeff feel as though he were walking on clouds. "Oh, Dad, can we go get him now?"

"I'll take you over in my car," the janitor offered. "We'll just about be in time to make the ferry that leaves at two o'clock."

The janitor's car moved more slowly than any car Jeff was ever in. He was sure they would never get to their destination. But finally they pulled into a driveway. David Oliver was an English boy about Jeff's age. He came running from the house as soon as his uncle's car stopped. At his heels bounced the most adorable ball of black fur Jeff had ever seen.

Soon they were all seated in the Olivers' living room with David and his mother. Jeff tried to hold the puppy but he squirmed to get down, and ran to David who squeezed him lovingly and explained, "I don't know what I'd do without Midnight. He's the only dog I've ever had."

Then his Uncle Pete reminded David how he got Midnight. He ended his story with, "So you see, young fella, I'm sure Midnight is Jeff's dog and he's come to take him home."

David pulled the pup close to his chest. His eyes filled with tears. "But Uncle Pete,"

Jeff watched David hold the dog close to him. That was supposed to be his dog, but David had saved its life . . .

he protested. He turned to Jeff and said, slowly, "I guess you want him as much as I do."

Suddenly, Jeff felt as though he had tumbled off his cloud and landed with a terrible thud. Midnight was supposed to belong to Jenny and him, but David had saved the puppy's life by caring for him when he was lost. David loved the beautiful puppy and it was obvious that Midnight returned his love.

Jeff turned to his father. He swallowed hard. "You know, Dad," he said in a voice that sounded strange to his own ears, "I don't think Midnight is our puppy. As a matter of fact I'm sure of it!" Jeff pushed past his father and dashed to the car.

At home that night Rickey was obviously amazed. "Astro, I can't understand you. You mean to say that you left the pup with this kid — what's his name, David?"

"Yeah," answered Jeff who couldn't talk about it anymore.

Tears were escaping down Jenny's cheeks

but she reached for Jeff's hand. "We wanted our puppy awfully bad," she told Rickey. "But Jeff said that David already loves him. I think Midnight really is David's dog."

RICKEY'S DECISION

JENNY SIGHED impatiently. She was so excited but there was nothing to do but sit and wait for the last high school basketball game of the season to begin. Rickey Welch was Rock County High's star forward. Mr. Loren, the jeweler who owned the store across the street from the school, along with some other business men, thought that Rock High's team could win the county championship this year. They offered some prizes to the center or forward who had top personal score at the end of the season! At the dinner table one night Rickey told the Rollins family how much he wanted to win the gold watch which was first prize.

"How come you're so quiet?" Jeff was waving his hand in front of his sister's face.

"I was just thinkin' about the night Rick told us about the contest," Jenny replied.

Jeff's eyes became serious. "I'll never forget him saying that his folks could never afford to buy him a watch because they wanted to stay and half starve in that dumpy little mission they were so crazy about."

Jenny put her elbows on her knees. "Yeah, I think Mom and Dad are still worried about Rick's attitude toward Jesus."

"I'm sure they are." Jeff sounded concerned himself. "You know, Rick seems to stop listening when we try to tell him about his need for Jesus. But I sure hope he wins that watch, and that Rock County wins the championship tonight."

The stands were nearly filled with spectators as the game's starting time drew closer. Mr. and Mrs. Rollins joined the twins.

"I saw the boys' points posted on a bulletin board downstairs," Mr. Rollins told Jeff and Jenny. "Rick and the other forward, Stanley White, are tied — 116 to 116. This is going to be the biggest game of the year all right."

"It sure is," agreed Jeff. Jenny nodded.

"It will determine the champion school team and the winners of the prizes," continued their father. "I sure hope Rick remembers to play teamwork and not just to make points for himself. It will be a big decision for the boy."

"Oh, dear!" Mrs. Rollins seemed worried. "Rick has been taken out of the other games several times by Coach Lovitt for failing to work with the team, hasn't he?"

"That's right, Evelyn. We'd better pray for him."

Jenny saw her mother bow her head right

then. Jenny knew she was praying for Rickey.

"Hey, everybody, they're ready for the toss!" yelled Jeff.

"Daddy!" screamed Jenny above the noise of the crowd. "Stanley is playing but Coach Lovitt is leaving Rick out of the game! Stanley will make more points than Rick!"

"The coach will put Rick in soon," her father assured her.

The game between Rock County and Waterton was so close the roof seemed to rise with the shouting of the crowd each time the ball slid through a basket. The half was three minutes from the finish when Rickey was waved into the game. The score stood at Rock County, 34; Waterton High, 37. Stanley was *six* points ahead of Rickey and Waterton was *three* points ahead of Rock County!

Rickey took his place. Seconds later the ball was in his hands, then falling through the rim without touching it. The score was changed to Waterton, 37; Rock County, 36.

Jenny squealed, "I knew Rick would win if the coach would let him play! Stanley is only four points ahead of him now!"

But on the next play it was Stanley who was closest to the basket. Rickey had the ball.

"Give it to Stan!" Mr. Rollins yelled.

But Rickey dribbled, then sent the ball to the center man. His basket went wide and Waterton took the ball!

"Dad, did Rick . . ." Jeff turned to his father.

"We can't say, Jeff," Mr. Rollins answered the unfinished question. "Only Rick knows why he threw the ball the way he did. Maybe he didn't know Stanley was closer to the basket."

Waterton failed to make their point and the Rock County team was able to end the half by making one more basket. The score was Rock County, 38; Waterton, 37. The third quarter and most of the fourth were dizzy ones for both teams.

*The crowd was going wild.
Would Rickey shoot for the
basket. Or would he throw the
ball to his teammate?*

There was one minute left to play. The score was tied at Rock County, 78; Waterton, 78. Rickey was tied with Stanley, too. Both boys had 122 points. It was Rock County's ball!

"We *have* to make one more basket!" screamed Jenny bouncing up and down.

"They'll use the old criss-cross," Jeff explained. "Rick told me they always do when they're in a tight spot."

"Then Rick will probably make one more basket. Rock County will win the game and he will win the watch, won't he, Daddy?" asked Jenny.

"That depends on the kind of criss-cross, Jenny." Her father looked serious. "It might be Stanley who will be in position to win or lose."

As the boys started to play again the center tipped the ball to Stanley, who came in ahead of a frantic Waterton guard. Rickey crossed over, whirled suddenly, found an opening and Stanley shot the ball to him. The spectators shrieked. Rickey dribbled to elude an opponent. He looked for the basket.

"Shoot!" yelled the onlookers.

One of the timers raised a gun without taking his eyes from his watch.

Rickey bent his knees, and took deliberate aim. "Why doesn't he hurry?" Jenny couldn't contain her anticipation. "What's the matter with him?"

The people gasped as Rickey finally released the ball. He threw it, however, not toward the basket but to someone underneath it, who flipped the ball upward and back. It slid through the meshes of the basket and the timer's gun sounded! There was a thunderous uproar!

The scorekeeper marked the final numbers — Rock County, 80; Waterton 78! "The boy came through, Evelyn!" Mr. Rollins squeezed his wife's hand.

"But, Daddy!" Tears streamed down Jenny's face. "That was Stanley who made the last basket. Rickey lost the watch, and he wanted it so badly."

"Yes, Miss Priss," Mr. Rollins replied. "Rick lost the watch but he proved to be man enough to sacrifice his own desires in order to win the game for the school and that kind of decision takes courage."

THE LOST
IS FOUND!

THE DAY the revival meetings were to begin at Calvary Church the Rollins family and Rickey were sitting at the breakfast table.

"Boy, we've waited so long for these meetings," exclaimed Jenny, "I can hardly believe the first one is tonight."

Rickey glared at Jenny.

Jeff set his glass of milk on the table thoughtfully. "I'm going to do my homework before dinner every night so I won't have to miss anything."

Rickey looked up quickly from his plate to Jeff's face. "You really mean that, don't you, Astro? You really *want* to go to those meetings?"

"Of course, don't you?" Jeff was finishing his egg and looking at the clock at the same time.

Mr. Rollins glanced up at Rickey. "You will be going to the meetings with us tonight won't you?" he asked.

Rickey shifted in his chair uneasily. "Well, I can't say now, Uncle Chris. I doubt if I can get my homework done in time."

Jenny's eyes sparkled with mischief. "You ought to be able to get it done as fast as Greta does hers," she challenged. "Cara Lee said their whole family will be there every night."

"Greta is going?" Rickey's question sounded involuntary and eager.

Mrs. Rollins smiled at her nephew. "Why not call Greta and see if she would like to make it a date?" she suggested.

Jeff and Jenny, along with their parents, arrived at the church early and met with others for prayer. When the twins came outside for a few minutes before time for the service, they were delighted to see Rickey driving up in their father's Volkswagen, and Greta was with him.

"Hi, kids," Greta greeted them warmly as she and Rickey started up the steps of the church.

"Are you two gonna' sit with us tonight?" Jenny invited.

Greta laughed and looked up at Rickey for approval. "Yeah, Twerp, we'd love to sit with you," he said with a wink at Greta.

The singing was so enthusiastic Jeff felt a tingly warmth run down his spine. He looked over at Rickey and saw that he was singing lustily. The evangelist began to speak.

His message was plain and forceful. Rickey seemed to squirm a lot and he looked uneasy. During the invitation he hung on to the back of the bench so tightly that his knuckles were white. He breathed a sigh of relief when the invitation was over and smiled down at Greta. Jeff heard him say, "Aunt Evelyn has some refreshments prepared and she invited us to join the family at the apartment — want to go?"

Mrs. Rollins had fixed a fluffy gelatin dessert which she served with cookies and hot chocolate. The family and the two teenagers were sitting around the kitchen table enjoying the dessert.

Greta remarked, "I was moved by the message tonight. It made me realize all over again how important it is to let other people know what Jesus has done for me."

Rickey looked at her quizzically.

Without looking at him, Greta continued. "I was in Junior High when I accepted the Lord," she said. "I know I would have done a lot of terrible things if I had not made my decision then. I have so much to be thankful for but lots of times I don't even mention the Lord to people."

When Greta asked Rick to tell her about when he was saved, he looked away. He didn't answer her for a long, long time.

Greta's voice was bubbling with enthusiasm as she turned to Rickey and asked, "How about you, Rick? You've never told me when you were saved. I'd like to hear about it."

An awkward silence followed. Jeff stared at Rick who kept his head down and turned a cookie over and over in his hand. Everyone looked at Rickey.

Finally, he turned to Greta and said nervously, "The reason I have never told you about trusting the Lord, Greta, is that I have never done it."

Jeff's heart pounded like a sledge hammer. He heard Greta gasp.

"But Rick," she mumbled, "your parents are missionaries." Her voice trailed off to a whisper.

Rickey continued as though he had not heard her. "All my life I've listened to my dad and mother talk about the Lord and what He meant to them. And, all my life I have thought only of the things that we had to do without that other people had who were not Christians. I made up my mind a long time ago that I was not going to be a Christian. I wanted to make plenty of money and buy the things we did without."

Mr. Rollins leaned forward across the table toward the youth. "Rick, you said you *wanted* to make money. Does that mean you feel differently now?"

Rickey dropped his head in his hands. "Yes, Uncle Chris. I think it was Astro and Twerp that convinced me."

Jeff and Jenny exchanged surprised looks. "But how, Rick?" asked Jeff.

The boy ran his fingers through his hair and answered without looking up. "When we went skiing you saved that woman's life after she treated you terribly. When you found out I was smoking you never called me down. Then you gave your puppy to another kid — because you thought he loved it. Now, I know that there's more to being a Christian than doing without things. To top it off, Greta came along. She made me realize I am a sinner. Uncle Chris, I'd like to be the kind of Christian Greta and the twins are."

Under Mr. Rollins' direction Rickey prayed, asking Jesus to come into his life and save him from sin. When he finished Mrs. Rollins hugged him, saying, "Oh, Rick, I wish your own parents could have been here tonight. Your decision would make them so happy."

Mr. Rollins began searching frantically in his pockets. "How could I have forgotten?" he mumbled. "Rick, this letter from Chile came to the office in care of me. I'm sorry I didn't give it to you earlier."

Rickey reached for the letter, his face white and drawn. He tore it open.

"They're *alive!*" he shouted.

His sentences were short and choppy as he tried to read and explain to the family at the same time. "Mom and Dad are both okay! They've been working in a make-shift hospital since the flood. They were cut off from communications—that's why we didn't hear from them!"

"Boy, Rick," Jeff exclaimed, "it seems like your whole family has been lost—but now you're *all* found!"

VICTORIA!

THE DOORBELL rang. Jenny glanced at her watch and pulled the brush through her hair. "Only eight o'clock! Who would come to the door at *that* time in the morning?" she wondered.

"Rick, it's a package for you!" Jeff yelled.

The whole family gathered around Rickey who read aloud the name on the return. It was a package from his parents!

Jenny could hardly wait to see inside.

"Open it quick!" she cried.

Rickey sat down on the couch, grinned at her, then slowly and deliberately began to tear the paper.

"Rickey Welch, you're teasing me!" she exclaimed. Everyone laughed—even Jenny.

Finally, Rickey pulled open the top. His eyes widened with pleasure. "Wow-w-w," he breathed, "Uncle Chris, *look!*" He held up a beautiful gold watch.

Mrs. Rollins moved closer to him on the couch and exclaimed, "Oh, Rick, it's lovely! Is there a letter?"

A note had been folded and stuffed underneath the watch. Rickey opened it and began to read aloud.

"Rickey, my son,
I received this watch as a token of love
from the people here in Chile. They gave
it to me because your mother and I have
been helping them to begin life again
after the devastating flood. I really
didn't deserve the gift and the people
gave it to me even though they couldn't

afford it. When I realized how valuable it was I wanted you to have it. I am giving it to you, my son, with my love.
Sincerely,
Your Dad."

Rickey looked up from the note to the faces of the people that were close to him, but said nothing.

"Oh, Rick," Jenny began, "that watch is lots better than the one you could have won." Her eyes shone and danced with joy.

"It sure is, Twerp." Rickey slipped his arm around her and squeezed hard. Then Mrs. Rollins tenderly kissed him on the cheek. Jeff and Mr. Rollins shook hands with the youth and Jenny thought she saw tears in her father's eyes.

That night the twins stayed after school to work on the latest issue of the school newspaper. It was dark when they started home. A street light above them came on as a sleek blue Imperial slid up to the curb next to the twins! A woman stuck her blonde head out the window and called, "Hey, you two, aren't you Jeff and Jenny Rollins?"

The twins stopped short! Jenny saw the woman's face in a beam of light. "Eva!" she exclaimed, running to the car. "How are you?"

The blonde woman laughed loudly. Jenny shrank involuntarily from the harsh voice and imposing attitude. She noticed that the driver of the car was someone she had never seen before. He was not the man who had been in the cafeteria with Eva.

Jeff came closer. Eva smiled.

"They told me at the hospital that you two kids saved my life by getting the Ski Patrol after my accident," she said. "I'm still walking with these crutches but I'll be as good as new soon." She reached out and patted Jenny's hand.

Jenny saw the crutches propped on the seat beside Eva.

"I intended to look you up later but now I won't have to. How much do I owe you kids?" the woman asked. "You name the amount. I'll give you a check."

Jeff and Jenny looked at one another in surprise. Jeff was first to find his tongue. "You don't owe us anything!" he exclaimed. "Anybody would have done the same thing."

"*Anybody* would not!" Eva corrected him sharply. "My boy friend didn't, and he was with me when that rock got in my way. I haven't heard from him since."

Jenny hesitated a moment then said, "But Eva, I'm sure anyone who was a *Christian* would have helped you."

Eva threw her head back and laughed uproariously while Jeff and Jenny watched her in bewilderment. "You mean you think religious people are different?" she scoffed. Gaining control of herself she continued. "I don't understand you two, but I guess religion is a good thing for kids. Here, let me at least do this for you." Eva searched through her large black handbag.

Jeff bent slightly to gain her attention again. "It's a good thing for anybody to know Jesus as Saviour," he said.

Eva looked up at him. "Now, don't you go trying to tell me I need Jesus." She laughed again. "Here," she said, reaching for Jeff's jacket pocket and stuffing something into it which she had taken from her purse. She turned to Jenny. "You, too," she said, motioning Jenny toward her. Jenny stepped closer to the car and Eva put something in her pocket.

The twins watched as the car sped away. They both reached into their pockets. Their eyes widened as they examined the two twenty dollar bills Eva had given them.

"Wouldn't it be awful to go through life without Jesus?" Jeff asked as they started home.

"Yeah," Jenny responded, "or to think your money can get you *anything.*"

Their talk with Eva left the twins depressed. They continued home in silence. Jeff opened the door and held it for his sister.

"Hello, we're home!" Jenny called to her mother as they usually did when returning from school.

No one answered.

"Jeff, did you hear a funny noise?" she asked.

Suddenly, the kitchen door flew open and a black bundle of fluff came tumbling toward them! "It's a *puppy!*" yelled Jeff.

Jenny gathered the tiny wriggling body close. The puppy licked her cheek. Jeff bent close to them and the puppy nosed his cheek too, as if to say, "I'm going to love *both* of you."

It was several moments later when the twins realized their mother was standing in the kitchen doorway, watching. "Grandpa and Grandma Rollins sent her when they found out you gave Midnight to David," Mrs. Rollins began. "She was the smallest pup in the litter. Grandpa was afraid she would not be healthy. But after his examination, Doc Hamilton pronounced her sound. So, she's *your* puppy."

Tears of happiness streamed down the faces of the twins. Jenny looked up at Jeff.

The cute puppy licked Jenny's face. "What will we name her?" she asked. Jeff knew just the right name for her.

"What should we call her?" she asked.

"Let's name her *Victoria,*" he answered. "Because that's where David and Midnight live. If it hadn't been for them we wouldn't have her!"

Jenny looked down at the little puppy and spoke as though she would understand. "We'll take you with us when we go to the mountains exploring during Spring vacation. Won't that be fun, Victoria?"

Have you read about
   Jeff's dog down in the well—
   Jenny's snake bite on the mountain trip—
   Halloween adventures?
Find all this excitement and more in

Jeff   and   Jenny

on   the   Chinchilla   Ranch.